# The Tale
# of Kimmy-Cat

## and The Frightened
## Teddy Bear

illustrated by
Maureen Bradley

AWARD PUBLICATIONS LIMITED

# The Tale of Kimmy-Cat

There was once a cat called Kimmy-Cat who loved going fishing. He fished in his master's goldfish bowl and caught six little goldfish and ate them. He was told off for that, but *he* didn't care! He just waited till more fish were put in the bowl and then he fished for those and ate them too!

Then he found his way to the neigh-
bour's pond, and waited patiently by the
water until a very big and beautiful fish
came by. Out went Kimmy-Cat's paw,
and the poor fish was caught and eaten.

Kimmy got into trouble for that, too.
The other cats laughed at him.

'Fancy going fishing!' they said. 'You
*are* a silly, Kimmy-Cat! Why, you have
nice fresh fish cooked for you every day,
and yet you go catching those poor goldfish. We think you are a naughty cat.'

'Goldfish taste so nice,' said Kimmy-Cat. 'You just come with me and taste them.'

But none of the other cats would do such a naughty thing. So Kimmy-Cat had to go alone. He didn't dare to go to the pond next door, so he roamed away by himself to look for another one.

Soon he came to a wood, and right in the very middle of it he found a perfectly round pond with pink waterlilies growing on the surface.

But better than waterlilies to Kimmy-Cat was a big fish, very golden, and with bright diamond-like eyes. It swam slowly about the little pond, and shone like gold.

'Ho!' said Kimmy-Cat to himself. 'That's the fish for me!'

He crouched down and waited until the fish came near the bank. Then in a flash he shot out his paw and caught it. It landed on the bank and wriggled to get away from him. But Kimmy-Cat got its tail into his mouth, and was just going to start eating the fish when a voice shouted at him:

'Leave that fish alone! You wicked cat, drop that fish at once!'

Out of a little cottage came a small man in red with a pointed cap on his head.

Kimmy-Cat saw that he was very tiny, so he took no notice of him. But the little man ran up to him and took the fish away. He slipped it into the water and it swam off, none the worse for its adventure.

'You bad cat!' said the little man. 'Haven't you been taught not to go fishing? It's as bad as stealing, to go fishing in other people's ponds. That goldfish is my pet, and I've had it for twenty years.'

'I've a good mind to sit here and catch it again,' said Kimmy-Cat.

Suddenly the little man looked closely at Kimmy-Cat's tail – and then he began to laugh and dance about in glee!

'Ho-ho!' he shouted. 'You've eaten a tiny bit of my fish's tail, and won't you be sorry for it! My fish is magic and you'll be sorry you ever touched it! Ho-ho!'

Kimmy-Cat looked at his tail. Then he looked again – and, oh dear me, whatever was this? His own tail was vanishing and he was growing a fish-tail instead!

Kimmy-Cat looked at it in horror. Even as he watched it grew bigger and bigger. At last his own tail was completely gone – and in its place was a fine fish-tail, golden bright and double-pointed.

'Oh my!' said Kimmy-Cat in dismay. 'What a dreadful thing! Here, little man, change it back at once!'

## THE TALE OF KIMMY-CAT

'I can't!' said the little man, still capering about in delight. 'No one can take it away for you, because it's magic. You'll have to go on wearing it – and every fish you eat will make it grow bigger still!'

Kimmy-Cat gave a loud miaow and ran away in fright. This was the worst thing that had ever happened to him! He ran all the way home and curled himself up in his basket before any of the other cats could see him.

But they smelt his fish-tail and came crowding round him, thinking he had got a fish in his basket. The dogs came too, and so did the cook.

'Have you got a fish there?' she said sharply. 'You know that the master forbade you to go fishing any more, you naughty cat. Get up and let me see if you have a fish!'

But Kimmy-Cat wouldn't move. He didn't want anyone to see his fish-tail. The cook suddenly became cross, tipped him out of his basket – and then stared in the greatest surprise at his tail!

'Good gracious, what's this?' she cried. 'Why, what have you done to your tail, Kimmy? It's a fish-tail!'

All the cats and dogs sniffed at it, and then they began to laugh.

'Ho, Kimmy's turning into a fish because he catches so many!' they said. 'Look at his tail! He's half a fish!'

Kimmy-Cat went very red indeed. He curled up in his basket again and pretended to take no notice. But soon more cats came up and more still, all attracted by the fishy smell in Kimmy-Cat's basket. In despair Kimmy-Cat jumped out and ran away.

But that was no use either – for wherever he went the cats nearby smelt fish and ran after him. How Kimmy-Cat wished he had never gone fishing!

At last he went back to the little man and begged for his help.

'I couldn't help you even if I wanted to, which I don't,' said the little man. 'The best thing you can do is to hide away until your own tail has grown again. It will take about a month, I should think.'

'But where can I hide?' asked poor Kimmy-Cat.

'Well, you can hide in my little house here, if you like,' said the man. 'But in return for that you must do all the work in my house for me. That will be very good for you, for I can see that you have thought of nothing and nobody but yourself up till now. You are too fat, besides being disobedient and unkind.'

Kimmy-Cat said nothing. He at once went indoors and found an apron to put on. Then he took a broom and began to work hard.

His own tail began to grow again. It gradually pushed the fish-tail away, and at last, by the time the month was nearly up, there was nothing left of the fish-tail except for a tiny spike at the end of his own furry tail. Kimmy-Cat was so glad. He had learnt a lot. He was a different cat when he said goodbye to the little man and went home again.

'Here comes Kimmy!' cried all the other animals. 'Where have you been, Kimmy-Cat? Where's your fish-tail?'

'It's gone,' said Kimmy-Cat. 'Please don't talk of it to me, my friends. I am a good cat now, and all I want is to be kind and friendly.'

'We will be nice to you!' said the cats and dogs at once. 'If you will be nice to us, we will never say a word about the fish-tail, not one! Come and have some cream! And there's some nice boiled fish that cook has got ready for us.'

'I'd like the cream – but not the fish!' said Kimmy-Cat with a shudder. And I'm not surprised, are you?

# The Frightened Teddy Bear

Once upon a time, Jane took her teddy bear out shopping and carried him all the way because he was not very big.

On the way home the little girl's shoe came undone, and she popped the bear down on a nearby step and did it up. But, oh dear me, when she stood up and went on her way again, she quite forgot to take her little bear!

# THE FRIGHTENED TEDDY BEAR

There he sat on the doorstep of a strange house, lost and alone. He saw Jane running away in the distance, and watched for her to turn back and fetch him – but she didn't. She had remembered that there was chocolate pudding for dinner and was running home as fast as she could.

Then a large sandy cat came along and looked at the bear.

'What are you doing here?' asked the cat. 'That is my doorstep you are sitting on. How dare you?'

'I'm very sorry,' said the little bear, getting up in a hurry. 'I really didn't know. My owner left me here.'

'Well, just remove yourself,' said the cat, sitting down and curling its big tail round its body. 'I've no use for bears.'

The sandy cat put out its paw and gave the teddy a sharp push. He fell down the step on to his nose, and then, afraid that the cat would scratch him, he jumped to his feet and hurried down the road.

Two boys and a girl suddenly saw him and stopped in surprise.

'Ooh, look!' said the girl. 'A bear walking all by himself.'

'Let's catch him!' cried the boys, and they all set off after the bear in a hurry. He was very frightened and began to run. The children tore after him and down the street they all sped, the little bear a good way ahead.

He puffed and panted and felt sure that they would soon catch him. He came to the corner of the road and ran round it. Just near-by was a baker's van, the back door of which was open, showing all the loaves there. The little bear suddenly gave a jump and landed among the loaves. Then he hid there, crouching behind a big currant loaf.

The three children turned the corner and were astonished to see that the bear had vanished.

'Where's he gone?' they said, standing so close to the baker's van that the little bear was afraid they would see him.

'Perhaps he's run into one of the gardens,' said the little girl. 'Let's look into each one and see.'

So down the street they went, peeping into each garden. Soon they were out of sight and the bear heaved a big sigh.

# THE FRIGHTENED TEDDY BEAR

He was just going to scramble out of the van when the baker came for his loaves, and put his hand in to get the big currant loaf. He saw the little bear and cried out in surprise.

'Oh, my!' he said. 'Whatever's this?'

The bear leapt out of the van, and then took to his heels and ran. The baker made a grab at him and missed. Then, full of surprise at the sight of a running teddy bear, he put down his basket and chased after him.

The bear ran on and on, hearing the baker just behind him. Then suddenly the man slipped and fell, and by the time he had picked himself up again the little bear had gone.

He had run down a little pathway and come to a field of buttercups. He flung himself down on the grass and panted, for he was really out of breath. 'Whatever shall I do?' he wondered. 'I am quite lost. Oh dear, I do feel miserable.'

# THE FRIGHTENED TEDDY BEAR

Two large tears came into his boot-button eyes and trickled down his furry brown nose – but, dear me, he hadn't time even to cry, for at that moment up came a large black dog, and sniffed hard at the frightened bear.

Teddy jumped to his feet in dismay. What a dreadful creature! Would it eat him? He saw what large, strong teeth the dog had, and once more the little bear began to run.

He ran through the golden buttercups, and the dog ran after him. But this time the little bear could not run very fast for he was tired. He looked back and saw that the dog would soon catch him up.

'Oh, what shall I do?' he groaned. 'I shall certainly be eaten if I am caught!'

Now just at that moment the bear saw an old kite lying on the grass. It had once belonged to a little boy who had flown it on a very windy day. The wind had broken the string and the kite had flown off by itself, coming to rest in the field, where it had lain for many days.

'Oh, kite!' cried the little bear, running up to it. 'Please, please, help me! Take me away from this horrid big dog!'

# THE FRIGHTENED TEDDY BEAR

The bear held on to the tail of the kite, which suddenly rose in the air, taking its unusual little passenger with it. The dog stopped in amazement, and then tried to jump up and snap at the bear – but the kite was now too high, and the dog was soon left behind.

The bear hung on to the tail for all he was worth, and the kite sailed steadily through the air.

'I shall have to come down in a minute,' said the kite. 'The wind is dropping, and I can't fly without wind, you know.'

The wind dropped, and the kite dropped too. Down it went and down, and soon it lay quietly on the grass in someone's garden. A little girl came running from the house to see what it was – and goodness, wasn't the teddy bear astonished to see her!

## THE FRIGHTENED TEDDY BEAR

It was Jane, his little owner, who had left him behind by mistake!

'Oh, the kite has brought my teddy back to me!' cried Jane, picking him up and hugging him. 'Oh, you dear little bear! I thought I had lost you for ever, for when I went back to look for you, you were gone! Oh, how lovely to see you again! And how kind of the kite to bring you! It's a dirty old thing, but it shall live in the nursery, because I'm so glad it brought you back again!'

# THE FRIGHTENED TEDDY BEAR

So the kite went upstairs with the teddy bear, who was delighted to be safe home once more. All his friends were pleased to see him again, and weren't they surprised to hear the tale of his adventures! As for the kite, he was quite a hero, and he and the teddy bear were fast friends for ever.

ISBN 0-86163-774-7

Text copyright Darrell Waters Limited
Illustrations copyright © 1995 Award Publications Limited

Enid Blyton's signature is a trademark of Darrell Waters Limited

*The Tale of Kimmy-Cat* first published 1951 by Pitkin
*The Frightened Teddy Bear* first published 1949 by Pitkin

This edition first published 1995 by Award Publications Limited,
27 Longford Street, London NW1 3DZ